# FIVE LITTLE DUCKS

# North-South Books

NEW YORK / LONDON

# Five Little Ducks

AN OLD RHYME · ILLUSTRATED BY

Pamela Paparone

Published in the United States by North-South Books Inc., New York.
Published simultaneously in Great Britain, Canada, Australia, and
New Zealand in 1995 by North-South Books, an imprint of
Nord-Süd Verlag AG, Gossau Zürich, Switzerland.

Library of Congress Cataloging-in-Publication Data
Paparone, Pamela.
Five little ducks: an old rhyme/ illustrated by Pamela Paparone.
Summary: When her five little ducks disappear one by one,
Mother duck sets out to find them.
1. Nursery rhymes. 2. Children's poetry.
[1. Nursery rhymes. 2. Ducks—Poetry. 3. Counting.] 1. Title.
PZ7.P196Fi   1995
95-13136

A CIP catalogue record for this book
is available from The British Library.

The artwork was created with acrylic paint and colored pencil
Designed by Marc Cheshire

ISBN 1-55858-473-0 (TRADE BINDING)
1 3 5 7 9 TB 10 8 6 4 2
ISBN 1-55858-474-9 (LIBRARY BINDING)
1 3 5 7 9 LB 10 8 6 4 2
Printed in Belgium

*To J.O. with love*

Five little ducks went out one day,
Over the hills and far away.

Mother duck said,
"Quack, quack, quack, quack."
But only four little ducks came back.

Four little ducks went out one day,
Over the hills and far away.

Mother duck said,

"Quack, quack, quack, quack."

But only three little ducks came back.

Three little ducks went out one day,
Over the hills and far away.

Mother duck said,

"Quack, quack, quack, quack."

But only two little ducks came back.

Two little ducks went out one day,
Over the hills and far away.

Mother duck said,
"Quack, quack, quack, quack."
But only one little duck came back.

One little duck went out one day,
Over the hills and far away.

Mother duck said,

"Quack, quack, quack, quack."

But none of the little ducks came back.

Sad mother duck went out one day,
Over the hills and far away.

Mother duck said,

"Quack, quack, quack, quack."

And all of her five little ducks came back!